IF YOUR BABYSITTER IS A BRUJA

TO MY KIDS, JOÃO FELIPE, LUIS EDUARDO, AND KARINA, WHO ALWAYS KEPT ME FLYING ON BROOMS AND BELIEVING IN MAGIC —A. S.

FOR ALL THE BRUJAS IN TRAINING —I. F.

Acknowledgments:
Many thanks to Marianna Llanos, who helped me with translations and who is an amazing author in her own right. She transformed a babysitter into a magical niñera who will fly into Spanish speakers' hearts. —A. S.

SIMON & SCHUSTER BOOKS FOR YOUNG READERS
An imprint of Simon & Schuster Children's Publishing Division
1230 Avenue of the Americas, New York, New York 10020
Text © 2022 by Ana Siqueira
Illustration © 2022 by Irena Freitas
Book design by Chloë Foglia © 2022 by Simon & Schuster, Inc.

SIMON & SCHUSTER BOOKS FOR YOUNG READERS and related marks are trademarks of Simon & Schuster, Inc.
For information about special discounts for bulk purchases, please contact Simon & Schuster Special Sales at 1-866-506-1949 or business@simonandschuster.com.
The Simon & Schuster Speakers Bureau can bring authors to your live event.
For more information or to book an event, contact the Simon & Schuster Speakers Bureau at 1-866-248-3049 or visit our website at www.simonspeakers.com.
The text for this book was set in Caslon 224.
The illustrations for this book were rendered digitally.
Manufactured in China
0522 SCP
First Edition
10 9 8 7 6 5 4 3 2 1
Library of Congress Cataloging-in-Publication Data
Names: Siqueira, Ana, author. | Freitas, Irena, illustrator.
Title: If your babysitter is a bruja / Ana Siqueira ; illustrated by Irena Freitas.
Description: First edition. | New York : Simon & Schuster Books for Young Readers, [2022] | Audience: Ages 4-8. | Audience: Grades K-1. | Summary: "If you get a new babysitter, and it's almost Halloween, be wary . . . for she might just be a bruja!" —Provided by publisher.
Identifiers: LCCN 2020037653 (print) | LCCN 2020037654 (ebook) | ISBN 9781534488748 (hardcover) | ISBN 9781534488755 (ebook)
Subjects: CYAC: Witches—Fiction. | Hispanic Americans—Fiction.
Classification: LCC PZ7.1.S5695 If 2022 (print) | LCC PZ7.1.S5695 (ebook) | DDC [E]—dc23
LC record available at https://lccn.loc.gov/2020037653
LC ebook record available at https://lccn.loc.gov/2020037654

OUR BABYSITTER IS A BRUJA

BY **ANA SIQUEIRA**

ILLUSTRATED BY **IRENA FREITAS**

SIMON & SCHUSTER BOOKS FOR YOUNG READERS
NEW YORK   LONDON   TORONTO   SYDNEY   NEW DELHI

If it's almost Halloween and you have a new babysitter . . . be wary.

She might be a bruja! A witch!

If she zooms in on a broom,
black sombrero on her head,
cackling like a crow . . .

¡¡CORRE!!
RUN!

But don't duck, drop, and roll.
The dust bunnies will tickle
your nose.

You'll

"ACHUUUUMMM!"

And she'll order her black cats to "Attack!"

¡AY, CARAMBA!

When you conquer los gatazos,
you will cook up a plan.

Garlic, sal, and hot fire.
Stir, mix, and
"bate, bate, chocolate."

You'll smile and offer,

"TRY MY
DELICIOSO DRINK."

She'll gobble it.
And . . .

¡AY, CARAMBA!

She'll spit it! She'll giggle. She'll cackle.

Your legs will tremble.
Your hands will shake.
You'll flee to the magic garden!

and drop you right there . . . The Twisted Torre!

And then
un plan perfecto.

You'll slither down the slimy slide.

The bruja will follow you and
PLOFT—
she'll be stuck there forever.

Fast, get her broom.
Without a broom, she'll lose all her power.

But somehow,

¡AY, CARAMBA!

She'll find a way to fly,
and catch up with you.

Then she'll dunk you in
a bubbling cauldron
with starving

¡¡¡COCODRILOS!!!

You'll escape. You'll sprint.

You'll remember . . .

the best defense against witches.

She'll storm from
the bathroom.

And you'll wish you
hadn't done that.

She was kind of fun after all.
You'll whisper, "Sorry."
And . . .

"Amiga, do you want
some Pan de Muerto?"
The bruja will grin.

¿PAN DE MUERTO?

Who can resist it?

Besides, she
called you amiga.
So here's what
you should do:

Write BFF on your
hand and hers.

Let her crown you
bruja-in-training and

POOFT!

Make magic potions.
Kiss frogs.

Even gobble up
zombie eyeballs.

¡DELICIOSO!

When your eyes can't stay open, take her to your enchanted tower.

She'll cast a sleeping spell that nobody can resist.

And if your babysitter zooms away
on a broom, black sombrero on
her head, cackling like a crow,
she's definitely a bruja, a good one.

JUST LIKE YOU.